MY AMERICA

My Brother's Keeper

Virginia's Diary

by Mary Pope Osborne

Scholastic Inc. New York

Gettysburg, Pennsylvania
1863

June 20, 1863

Here begins the writing of Virginia B. Dickens, sister of Jedidiah Dickens who has trusted her with the keeping of his journal, as he has gone to help our Uncle Jack hide his horses from Confederate raiders who roam the countryside.

I, Virginia B. Dickens, am sitting on top of Cemetery Hill in the town of Gettysburg, in the State of Pennsylvania.

Songbirds.
Gravestones.
Blue sky.
Green grass.

Later

I do not know what else to say.

I have been sitting here on Cemetery Hill for half an hour.

Jed told me that I am to write what I hear and what I see. He told me to write what I truly feel and truly think. Above all, Jed said, be honest.

Well, to be honest, I don't think I have heard or seen anything worth writing about.

All I hear are birds singing the same songs over and over.

All I see are old tombstones. One of them has my mother's name on it.

What do I truly feel?

Right now I truly feel a little angry at Jed and Pa for going to Uncle Jack's without me.

Pa said he did not want to put me in harm's

way. So I am to stay at Reverend McCully's for a few days, until Pa and Jed get back.

For goodness sakes, Pa! I am nine years old now! I do everything with you and Jed!

And what do I truly think?

What I truly think is this: I do not know how to keep this journal. Everything I have written so far is angry or foolish.

So good-bye for now.

Late at night

The McCullys are all asleep.

I am writing by candlelight in the attic room I share with Jane Ellen.

Jane Ellen is Reverend McCully's younger sister from Philadelphia. She is eighteen years old, the same as Jed. She has moved here only recently. After our summer recess, she will be the new school mistress at my school.

What do I truly feel right now?

To be honest, I feel a little angry at Jane Ellen.

Before she went to sleep, Jane Ellen asked me all sorts of questions about Jed.

I told her Jed loves to read and write. I told her he writes every day. While he is away, he wants me to write for him.

Jane Ellen said she also loves to read and write. Then she said I had a wonderful brother. She thought he was quite handsome, too.

If I was honest, I'd have to say I did not like hearing Jane Ellen praise Jed this way. She has only met him once — the day he brought me here. How could she know how wonderful he is?

June 21, 1863

I am sitting on top of Cemetery Hill.

I feel a bit guilty for not offering to help Mrs. McCully this morning.

When I left her house, she asked where I was going. I told her I had to go write in Jed's journal. She just nodded and told me to come back for the noon meal.

Mrs. McCully is too busy to pay much attention to my comings and goings. With three-year-old twins, a new baby, and Reverend McCully away in Philadelphia, she has more than enough to think about.

I know I should offer to help her. But Jane Ellen is there to do that. My job is to write in Jed's journal while he is away.

"Be my eyes and my ears in Gettysburg," he told me.

That is the biggest job I have ever had.

So, what do my eyes see for you right now, Jed? They see a wheat field, an apple orchard, and a cornfield. They see riders on horseback coming down Emmitsburg Road.

What do I feel?

If I was honest, Jed, I would have to say I feel sad. Sad because those riders are not you and Pa.

June 22, 1863

We heard frightening news this morning.

An old friend of Reverend McCully's came to visit. His name is Mr. Hoke. He works for a newspaper in Washington, D.C. He has come to Gettysburg to write a story about the Confederate army.

Mr. Hoke said thousands of Rebels are riding through Pennsylvania. They are coming very close to Gettsyburg!

Pa and Jed had better hurry back before all those Rebels get between them and home.

June 23, 1863

On the way to the store this morning, Mrs. McCully and I saw a number of Negro people hurrying down Baltimore Street. They all carried big bundles on their backs. The person leading the way was Becky Lee, the nice lady who helps Mrs. McCully with her wash.

Mrs. McCully shouted to Becky Lee, asking where she was going.

Becky Lee said the Rebs were coming! She said she was going to hide her children in the woods near Culp's Hill.

Mrs. McCully told her to come stay with us.

But Becky Lee said no house in Gettysburg was safe. She said the Rebs will search all the houses for Negroes and drag them south to be slaves.

Mrs. McCully opened her handbag and gave Becky Lee all her money. She told Becky Lee she would pray for her and her children.

What a terrible thing for people to be slaves. God created all people equal. But slavery treats some people like animals. Why, Becky Lee has to hide her children just like Uncle Jack has to hide his horses!

Mrs. McCully says if the Union wins the war, President Lincoln's wish will come true — there will be no more slavery in any states.

But she says the Union is not doing well. The Confederates have won many battles. If they win a big battle in Pennsylvania, she thinks they might win the whole war!

Later

My friends Sally and Betsy are leaving town, too. Their families are taking the last train out of Gettysburg in the morning. They will stay in York until the Rebels have come and gone.

Many people are leaving town. But Mrs. McCully said that we will not leave. She fears that if we leave, the Rebs might rob the house. The Rebs only rob empty houses, she says.

Then what about *our* empty house? Mine and Jed's and Pa's? It is sitting all by itself across town, with no one at all to guard it.

Uncle Jack's horses are important. But so is Pa's violin. And Mother's gold locket and pearl-handled hairbrush. What if the Rebs steal Jed's books? His plays by William Shakespeare, and *The Death of King Arthur?*

June 24, 1863

Mr. Hoke came to dinner again today. He said that right now the Rebs are spreading over the countryside just outside town!

He said it is now dangerous for ordinary citizens to travel to and from Gettysburg.

When I told Mr. Hoke about Pa and Jed, he said they should stay at Uncle Jack's until all the Confederates have left this area.

"Oh, yes! Jed should stay right where he is," Jane Ellen said with a look of great concern.

What I would like to know is: Why should Jane Ellen care so much about Jed's safety? Goodness, she hardly knows him.

I imagine Pa must feel bad about leaving me here. He said the Rebs would never come near Gettysburg. He said he was leaving me in the safest place in the world — a sleepy little farm town, not big enough to attract a fly.

How strange that I am the one in harm's way, while Pa and Jed are safe at Uncle Jack's farm.

What do I truly feel?

Maybe I truly feel just a tiny bit scared.

Late afternoon

I am sitting on Cemetery Hill, near my mother's grave.

There is something I keep wondering. If my mother had lived, would she be on the side of the Rebels now?

My mother was born in Virginia. She loved the state of Virginia. Why, right before she died, she told Pa to name me Virginia!

After my mother died, Pa lost touch with her family. But he once told me she had two younger brothers. What if they come to Gettysburg to fight our Union soldiers?

Jed says this war has torn apart many

families. He says President Lincoln is the only one who can make us one nation again.

June 25, 1863

I cannot stop thinking about my mother.

Pa says my mother was a beautiful Southern belle.

Pa always says this in a humble, shy way. It is as if he cannot figure why a beautiful Southern belle would leave Virginia and move to the North with him.

But that's easy to figure. Pa has bright crinkly eyes and music in his heart. Whenever he plays his violin, everyone feels happy. Why, anyone would follow Pa when he plays his violin!

I like to picture my mother in a flouncy pale dress, dancing barefoot to Pa's music. I can almost hear her tinkling laughter and see her dark curls.

I think she will always be young and beautiful in Pa's mind. Whenever he speaks about her, he sounds like he's telling a fairy tale.

If I told the Rebs such things about my mother, would they go away and leave our house alone?

Late evening

I saved our treasures!

I went to our house before nightfall. I lit a candle and put Jed's books in a satchel, along with Pa's violin and my mother's pearl-handled hairbrush.

I confess I am now wearing her gold locket. Pa would never let me wear it before. But surely it is better for me to wear my mother's locket than have it stolen by the Rebs.

Mrs. McCully praised my mission. She said

Pa and Jed would be proud of me. Then she hid the satchel in the cellar.

All evening Jane Ellen kept asking, "Where is our army?" She wonders if President Lincoln himself even knows where our army is. If he does, why is he letting the Confederates ride around our countryside, doing as they please?

I told Jane Ellen that President Lincoln is Jed's greatest hero in all the world. I told her that she mustn't speak ill of Mr. Lincoln when she is in my brother's presence.

Do you know what she did then?

She threw her hands across her heart and wailed, "I know. I love him, I love him desperately."

Why, Jane Ellen! Did you mean President Lincoln? Or my brother Jed?

June 26, 1863

The Rebels rode through Gettysburg this very day! At about two o'clock, we heard their yells. We heard whistles and drums.

When we peeked outside, what a sight we saw!

A Rebel band was playing in the Center Square! Hundreds of Confederates were passing by our house!

I could not look away, even when Jane Ellen urged me to close the shutters.

First the Rebs came on horses. Then they passed on foot. Some waved red flags. But they made a pitiful sight in their dirty, gray uniforms.

A man with his feet wrapped in rags called out howdy to me. Another asked how many Yankee soldiers were in town.

I shouted it was none of his business.

The Reb laughed a wild laugh. He told me

they were going to whip the Yankees no matter how many there were! Then he fired his pistol in the air and whooped.

Jane Ellen slammed the shutters closed.

Now it is raining hard. I am writing while Mrs. McCully and Jane Ellen bake bread.

We can hear the Rebs firing their pistols in the Square and yelling their Rebel yells.

If she were here right now, what would my mother feel? Her brothers could be part of that crowd. When I look at her picture in her locket, her tiny face seems sad.

Later

A little while ago, Mr. Hoke came by to make certain we were safe. He said the Confederates had met with the Gettysburg town council today. They demanded meat, shoes, and Yankee dollars. They threatened to burn down the whole town if they did not get what they wanted.

The council said they could go in the stores and take anything they could find, but they would not find much.

The worse news from Mr. Hoke was this: Some free Negro people who had stayed in town have been caught and taken away.

Mrs. McCully is worried sick that Becky Lee and her children might have been found in the woods. She says we must all pray for them.

Late night

We are in our beds now. We can still hear the Rebel yells coming from the square.

Jane Ellen and I both said special prayers for Becky Lee and her children.

Mrs. McCully told us that Becky Lee was

once a slave herself. She escaped from the South, and ever since then she has secretly helped other slaves escape. She slips over the Mason-Dixon line to Maryland and leads runaway slaves to freedom in the North.

Jane Ellen said Becky Lee is the bravest person she's every heard of.

Good night, Becky Lee. Good luck.

June 27, 1863

It is barely daylight, but Mrs. McCully is already baking bread.

That woman bakes bread all the time. She gives it free to anyone who needs it. She even gave a loaf to a hungry Reb who knocked on our door late last night!

Mrs. McCully seems to think that baking bread is the best way to hold the Union together.

Later

The Confederates have left Gettysburg! They left this morning without burning a single building.

Mrs. McCully says that if the Rebs keep moving north the train will start running again. Reverend McCully can return from Philadelphia. And Pa and Jed can ride back safely from Uncle Jack's farm!

I confess I hate to give you back your journal, Jed, as I am starting to like writing very much. But I would rather have *you* than your journal any day. That is what I truly feel.

Late night

It seems the Rebs have not gone very far away.

Mr. Hoke told us the Confederates have set

up camp just a few miles to the west and north of Gettysburg. So it is still not safe to travel from the countryside into town.

Will Pa and Jed never be allowed to come back to me? They have been gone for more than a week. That is the longest I have been separated from them in all my life.

If I am honest about what I feel, I must say I am close to tears.

June 28, 1863

What did I hear today? Good news!

At the candy store, Jane Ellen and I heard that a Union cavalry unit is only fifteen miles away.

Hurrah! Surely the cavalry will drive the Confederates away from our land. So Pa and Jed can finally return safely from Uncle Jack's.

June 30, 1863

We saw an amazing sight today.

General Buford's Union cavalry passed right through Gettysburg! There were so many riders on horseback, I could not count them.

The older girls handed out cakes and blew kisses at the parade. They seemed to fall in love with every soldier in blue who passed by.

Later

I am sad to say that the arrival of the Union soldiers has not frightened the Rebs away.

Tonight from our attic window, we can see campfires of the Confederates to the west, and we can see Union campfires twinkling to the south.

Mrs. McCully said we are headed for a big disaster indeed. She said two huge armies so close to each other can only mean a mighty storm is coming. And no one can do a thing to stop it.

July 1, 1863

We were baking bread this morning when the storm hit.

We heard cannon fire and galloping and yelling. Then two Union soldiers jumped onto our porch. Their faces were bloody!

They said fighting had broken out to the west, beyond Chambersburg Pike! They told us that the Union soldiers had been outnumbered. Many had been wounded. Now the Rebels were chasing them through town!

Mrs. McCully has taken the two soldiers down to the cellar.

Jane Ellen rocks both twins and the baby in her arms.

I am sitting on the stairway, writing as fast as I can. I am about to slip outside so I can see and hear what is happening for Jed.

Later

I am sitting in a tree in the Widow Thomas's front yard.

I have just seen terrible things:

People screaming in the streets.

Horses running wild.

~A bald soldier with his head covered in blood.

I almost ran screaming back to Mrs. McCully's house. But I knew Jed would want me to see and hear more. I prayed Mrs. McCully would not miss me. Then I flew the other way.

At the square, I turned onto Chambersburg Pike and ran toward the seminary.

When I got to the Widow Thomas's house, I saw a powerful sight.

In the fields below the seminary, thousands of Union soldiers were marching through the corn rows. Their guns gleamed in the light.

Rebs were lined up across from them.

The men looked like tiny toy soldiers. But they were firing!

I saw some Confederate riders galloping up the road. I ran to a tree and began climbing.

I climbed and climbed, like I was trying to get to heaven. My heart was beating so fast I almost fell.

Now, when I look out between the leaves, the fields are covered with thick smoke. I cannot see the soldiers anymore. I can only hear the roar of their cannons and gunfire.

I have made a terrible mistake. I am trapped here. Rebs continue to ride by below. I pray they will not see me. My hand shakes so badly I cannot write more.

Late afternoon

I am back at the McCullys' house. I cannot believe I am still alive.

I tried to climb down the tree a bit to hide myself better. But I slipped and fell to the ground.

Confederates were riding straight toward me!

I screamed in terror. A Rebel officer stopped his horse. He jumped from his saddle, grabbed me and asked where I lived.

I could not speak. I just pointed toward town.

He pulled me onto his horse and held me tightly and rode off.

I thought I had been captured!

When we got to the corner of High Street, he stopped and asked if I lived nearby.

My teeth were chattering so badly, I could not answer.

The Rebel got down off his horse, then helped me down, too. He took my hands and asked my name.

I told him my name was Virginia. Trembling all over, I told him to please not hurt me because my mother was a Southern belle. I opened her locket and showed him her tiny picture. I told him she was dead.

The officer smiled sadly at me. He said he would never hurt me. He told me his name was Captain Heath. He said he had a little girl about my age. Her name is Lily.

Captain Heath and his wife and Lily live in the North Carolina mountains. He and Lily like to pick blueberries together and look at the stars.

I said that sounded nice. I thought it truly did. I told him I hoped he saw Lily again soon.

Tears came to Captain Heath's eyes.

He said he wanted this war to end more than anything, so he could see his wife and Lily again. He asked me to pray for peace, and I said I would.

Then he said, "Run home, Virginia. God be with you."

I waved at him. Then I ran away as fast as I could.

When I got back to the McCullys', I found everyone in a state of shock. Confederates had dragged away the two Union soldiers hiding in the cellar.

Mrs. McCully was soothing the twins. They were screaming in terror.

Jane Ellen rocked the baby. Her face was

white as a sheet. When she saw me, she cried out, "Ginny, where have you been?"

"Up a tree," is all I said.

Late night

The Rebs are camped out on the sidewalks. They have captured the town.

Before we closed the shutters, we watched their ragged shadows under the bright moon. We listened to their wild talk. They sounded happy about the day's fighting. They said tomorrow they would whip the Yankees once and for all.

I cannot rest. In my mind, I still see the smoke in the fields and the bald man with blood on his head.

I keep thinking about Captain Heath.

Is he talking wild Rebel talk tonight? Or is he thinking of Lily instead?

I cannot tell anyone about him. But I know now that not all Confederates are bad people.

I pray that God ends this war, so Captain Heath can look at the stars with Lily again. I pray Pa and Jed and I can picnic near the pond again, and Pa can play his violin while a breeze makes the willows sway.

July 2, 1863

Since early morning, we have heard rifles popping. Everyone is jumpy.

Mrs. McCully has been baking bread night and day. A while ago, Mr. Hoke came by. He said that last night, nearly the entire Union army arrived! General Meade's army of the Potomac marched in by moonlight. They camped at the crest of Cemetery Hill and slept among the tombstones.

My mother's tombstone says, "May She Rest in Peace."

What must she think with soldiers camping on her grave?

Noon

Mrs. McCully wants Jane Ellen to take fresh bread to a hospital that has been set up in St. Francis Church. I have asked to go with her.

At first they both said I was too young. But I said that I am not too young. I should help, I said.

Mrs. McCully finally agreed I could go. Jane Ellen and I will leave as soon as the next loaves come from the oven.

Later

I am under my bed now. Under my own bed
in my own house.

This afternoon I did a terrible thing.

When Jane Ellen and I delivered our bread
to St. Francis Church, we found wounded men
lying in the aisles, moaning and crying out for
help. They had hymn books for pillows. The
hymn books were red with blood.

Doors had been laid across pews to serve as
operating tables. A surgeon saw me standing at
the back of the church and called me over.

A man with a bloody leg was lying there.
The surgeon held a saw. He said he needed me
to hold the man's hand while he sawed off the
man's leg.

The hurt man was very young. He had soft,
brown eyes.

I started to cry. I could not bear to see the

man get his leg sawed off. Blinded with tears, I ran out of the church.

Jane Ellen called to me. She even ran after me. But I ran faster.

I ran across town all the way to my old house.

I found the door broken down. No one was inside.

Robbers have been here. All our furniture is turned over.

I ran upstairs and hid under my bed.

I did not help the suffering man. I did not hold his hand. I ran like a coward.

Late afternoon

I am sitting at our old kitchen table. It is almost dark now. I fell asleep under my bed. I had a terrible dream of the surgeon and his saw. I woke up and found my way downstairs.

I am hungry. But the robbers took away all

our food — bags of flour and coffee and sugar. They took our cooking pots, too.

Evening

At twilight I heard voices cheering in the street.

I looked out the window and saw a group of Confederate officers. They were passing right by the house.

A bearded man in a neat, gray uniform led the way. His gaze rested on my window for a moment. He looked very handsome and dignified in the saddle.

I heard a soldier shout, "General Lee!" and the man looked away.

He must have been General Robert E. Lee himself, commander of the whole Confederate army!

Would my mother have loved Robert E.

Lee if she had stayed in Virginia? Like Jane Ellen and Jed love Abraham Lincoln?

July 3, 1863

It is early in the morning, before daylight.

I cannot stop thinking about the man in the hospital. I did not hold his hand. I did not comfort him.

I will always wonder if he lived. I will never forget what I did not do.

Dawn

A cloudy light now comes through the windows. Guns are firing in the distance.

I could not sleep all night. I was afraid of having bad dreams again.

I am so hungry.

I know Mrs. McCully and Jane Ellen must think very poorly of me now. They admire people who have courage, like Becky Lee. Not cowards like me who run away from helping others.

But I am desperate to go back. All I can think of is Mrs. McCully's freshly-baked bread.

Later

I am back in Mrs. McCully's house.

She and Jane Ellen were not scornful of me, not at all. When Mrs. McCully opened the door, she cried out, "Praise God!" and pulled me inside.

When Jane Ellen saw me, she said, "Oh, Ginny!" and burst into tears.

They said they had been terribly worried about me. They had even sent Mr. Hoke to search for me. They said he went in our house and looked in all the rooms, but could find no one.

I told them I had fallen alseep under my bed.

Mrs. McCully said she knew how badly I must miss my father and brother. She said she misses Reverend McCully, just like I miss Pa and Jed. But she knew they would all come home as soon as Gettysburg was free of Rebels. We must pray for their safe return, she said.

Then Jane Ellen took my hands. She said that I should not feel ashamed about what happened at the church.

She said she herself was horrified to see the wounded men get their limbs amputated. She said even the doctors were horrified, but that they had to deaden their feelings to do their work. She said that my running away showed my feelings are not dead. That is a good thing, she said. Then she put her arms around me.

I let Jane Ellen hug me for a very long time.

In this moment, Jed, I think it might be all right for Jane Ellen to be your sweetheart.

Noon

The cannons boom now in an unending roar. The baby is screaming. Mrs. McCully is stuffing cotton into his little ears to keep him from going deaf.

The whole house trembles and shakes. It feels like the end of the world.

Out the window, toward the south, the air is filled with clouds of smoke.

We know there is a great battle raging. But we do not know if it is our side or their side that is winning.

Evening

It is quiet now. A hard rain falls.

Mr. Hoke says the rain is a blessing. It will help wash away the blood of the thousands who died today.

Mr. Hoke told us he had spent the day witnessing a great battle.

He said that at three o'clock, thousands of Confederates marched out of the woods and started across the green fields south of town. A general named Pickett led them.

Mr. Hoke said the Confederates moved like a gray tide washing over the fields. But when they had cleared the fences, Union soldiers on Cemetery Hill and Round Top opened fire.

The Union men had been hiding behind rock walls. They killed thousands of General Pickett's soldiers.

Still, the Confederates kept coming. They

stepped over their dead and marched straight toward the shooters.

Mr. Hoke said the smoke from the cannons grew so thick that all was hidden from sight. He could hear the eerie Rebel yells over the gunfire, until an unearthly silence fell over the fields.

Then Union soldiers began cheering their victory from the summits of Cemetery Ridge and Round Top.

After night had fallen, a Union band played "Home Sweet Home." The simple, sad song wafted over the thousands of men who lay dead or dying in the dark fields.

Late night

The house shakes with a thunderstorm. Rain falls in buckets outside.

After Mr. Hoke left, Mrs. McCully began baking madly. Jane Ellen and I helped her. But

Mrs. McCully did not speak. We kneaded the dough in silence and slipped pan after pan into the oven.

While I baked, I thought of Captain Heath. Was he one of the Confederates who charged across the field? Did he fall with the thousands? Will he never pick blueberries with Lily again?

It was past midnight when Mrs. McCully stopped baking. She stared out the window at the dark storm. Then she spoke to me and Jane Ellen for the first time all evening.

Her voice shook. She told us that the rain fell so hard because the sky was weeping. She said a terrible thing had happened in Gettysburg these past three days.

Then she turned from us and began to weep.

Jane Ellen started crying. I did, too. I cried for Captain Heath and for all the dead men on the fields and streets. Union soldiers and Confederates.

Like the hard rain falling, we three wept over the terrible thing that has happened in Gettysburg.

July 4, 1863

Mr. Hoke came by after supper. He said General Lee's entire army had retreated. General Meade's Union army is leaving, too.

Later we heard town folks cheering the Union troops as they moved past our house. In the dark, we heard soldiers singing "The Star-Spangled Banner," and shouting "Hurrah!" for the Fourth of July.

Mrs. McCully told her twins that their father would come home now. She said that Jed and Pa would return soon, too. She said we must all still pray that the Lord will bring them back safely.

I am praying my heart out for Pa and Jed. I can hardly wait one more minute to see them.

July 5, 1863

All night I heard the wagons rolling out of town. It has grown quieter now.

At first light, Mrs. McCully went out and scrubbed the pavement in front of the house. Not even the hard rain had washed the blood away.

The smell in the air was terrible. Jane Ellen and I tied rags around our faces. Then we walked out and saw things almost too horrible to speak of.

The swollen bodies of men and horses were lying in the streets. The living wounded were crawling on the ground and moaning. There were flies everywhere. And vultures.

The smell was so bad Jane Ellen and I both vomited.

The bad odors have crept into the house now. Each of us carries a little bottle of peppermint oil.

July 6, 1863

What do I feel?

I feel sick.

I do not feel like writing any more of the corpses. Or of the sad cries of the dying and the bad smells. Or of the dead horses.

I hate this war.

I wish yesterday had been a beautiful Sunday, and that Pa, Jed, and I had gone to church together.

I wish we had then taken a ride to the countryside. Eaten a nice picnic with ham and apple pie.

I wish I had heard Jed read from *The Death of King Arthur*. I wish Pa had once again told his favorite story, the one he tells again and again. How my mother went to the theater in Richmond one night and saw him play his violin on stage.

Pa loves to tell how she waited for him afterward. How they danced together in the moonlight. How one day he talked her into running away with him, even though he was only a poor violin player.

Pa's sweet dream seems a million miles away from this world of death and terrible smells.

At twilight I tied a rag around my face and hurried through the streets to our house.

When I got there, it looked more empty than ever. Empty of life. Empty of our dreams.

July 7, 1863

Reverend McCully has returned!

He had been trying to get back for over a week. But just as Mr. Hoke told us, it was too dangerous to travel through Confederate lines.

Finally, after the Rebs started south, Reverend McCully hired a stage driver to drive him home.

Everyone shouted with joy when he came through the door. The twins clung to his legs.

Then we had another happy arrival. Becky Lee and her family! They are all safe and well, too!

We all sat down for hot rolls and coffee and gave thanks to the Lord for everyone's safe return.

If I was truly honest, I'd have to say I did not give thanks with *all* my heart. I am missing Pa and Jed too much.

But surely they will arrive next. Then I will give all my thanks. I will give great thanks forever.

July 8, 1863

Pa and Jed are still not back yet.

I visited our house just after sunrise. I thought perhaps they had returned last night. Perhaps they were planning to fetch me this morning.

But still no signs of life. When I got back to the McCullys', Mr. Hoke was here. He said as many as 20,000 wounded men have been left behind in Gettysburg. Now our small town of fewer than 2,500 people must care for them all.

He said there was a terrible need for food. Farmers must bring meat and vegetables from the countryside, or the citizens of Gettysburg and the wounded will all starve to death.

Later

I overheard the McCullys talking tonight.

Mrs. McCully said Pa and Jed should be home by now. She is most worried.

Reverend McCully said something must have happened to them.

Mrs. McCully said they must not let me know of their worries.

I feel angry at Mrs. McCully. She said if we prayed for Pa and Jed's safe return, the Lord would protect them! Why does she not have more faith in our prayers?

July 9, 1863

Still no sign of Pa and Jed.

Ten wounded Union soldiers sleep in the McCullys' house now. Every house in Gettysburg is crowded with the wounded.

All day Jane Ellen and I brought out quilts, old pillows, and rags to make beds.

Reverend McCully and Jane Ellen cut off the soiled uniforms. They bathed the soldiers. They dressed their wounds. They fear a man from Maine will die soon. He was shot in the throat.

Jane Ellen is a good nurse. She talks sweetly to the men.

Mrs. McCully and I care for the twins and baby. We have baked so many loaves of bread, we both have blisters on our hands.

The soldiers call us angels. Jane Ellen does indeed look like an angel, with her lovely wavy hair and big green eyes.

I think the soldiers are angels, too. They are kind and grateful and never complain.

I confess, though, I only give them part of my attention. The rest of me looks and listens all the time for Pa and Jed.

Later

There is more work to do than ever. The twins and baby are sick. Mrs. McCully says it's because of the bad odors from outside.

I am desperate to ask Reverend McCully to take me to Uncle Jack's farm, so I can find Jed and Pa. But I must be patient. Reverend McCully does not have a moment to spare.

July 10, 1863

The twins and baby are better today.

Farmers are streaming in from the countryside, bringing food to Gettysburg. They are giving out wagonloads of bread, ham, jellies, butter, potatoes, flour, cornmeal, salt pork, and clothes.

Are Pa and Jed bringing meat and

vegetables from Uncle Jack's farm? Is that why they are so late returning?

I asked this of Mrs. McCully. But she only sighed and said, "Perhaps, child."

I got a bit cross with her. I said that I was still praying to God, and I expected God to bring them back home safely!

"Of course, my dear," Mrs. McCully said. But she did not look at me when she said this.

July 11, 1863

At noon Jane Ellen and I went to collect food for our household from the Christian Commission.

We ran into Mr. Hoke. He said a great number of doctors and lady nurses were in town. They are moving the wounded from people's houses into hospitals.

Hospitals are everywhere — in churches, at the college, the seminary, and in the courthouse.

Mr. Hoke said there are field hospitals throughout the countryside, too. In farms and barns and schoolhouses. All are filled with wounded soldiers.

July 12, 1863

The house is hot. We must sleep with all the windows shut, as the air outside still smells very bad.

This morning, the wounded men at the McCullys' were moved to field hospitals. As soon as they were gone, other boarders arrived — people from far away who have come to Gettysburg to search for their lost loved ones.

Two women from New Jersey now camp in the parlor. They will look for their missing husbands.

A farmer from Massachusetts sleeps in the kitchen. He will visit the shallow graves in the fields. He hopes to find the remains of his three boys, so he can carry them home and bury them on his farm.

July 13, 1863

I have made up my mind. I am going to find my father and brother. I will get my satchel from the cellar. I will carry Pa's violin and Jed's books back to our house.

If they do not come home by tomorrow, I will start walking to Uncle Jack's.

Later

I am home.

This is the worst night of my life.

Pa came back. But Jed is missing.

I was in the cellar when I heard Pa calling. I rushed upstairs to greet him. I jumped into his arms. Then I asked where Jed was.

Pa looked confused. He said he had sent Jed back to Gettysburg a long time ago to take care of me.

I told him Jed had never arrived.

Pa nearly collapsed. He said something terrible must have happened to Jed. He said he had to look for him.

Pa told me to go back to the McCullys'. He said he would find Jed. Then he ran from the house, got on his horse, and started off.

I screamed after him. But Pa did not seem to hear me.

Evening

Reverend McCully came by to find out why I had not returned to their house.

While he was here, Pa came back. He was shivering and his eyes looked wild.

Reverend McCully calmed him down and made him explain what had happened.

Pa said that he and Jed had hidden Uncle Jack's horses. After that, Uncle Jack had hurt his back. So Pa stayed with him and sent Jed back to Gettysburg.

That was more than two weeks ago. Pa now fears Jed might have been caught in the fighting or captured by the Rebels.

Reverend McCully prayed with us for Jed's safe return.

After he left, I tried to comfort Pa. I opened my mother's gold locket and held up her tiny picture. I said she was keeping Jed safe for us.

Pa took the locket from me. Then he went to his room.

Now his door is closed. I can hear him pacing and talking to himself. I hear him telling my mother he is sorry.

I do not know what to do.

July 14, 1863

The McCullys are visiting with Pa now. They are in the parlor, praying for Jed.

What if I never see Jed again?

When my mother died, Jed was only nine years old. He and Pa both tried to be a mother to me. They sewed my clothes. They cooked for me. Before I even went to school, Jed taught me how to read and write.

How can I live without him?

July 15, 1863

Pa tried to chop wood this afternoon. But he could not work long. His hands were shaking too badly.

He has not touched his violin since he has been home. He says the music has left his heart.

July 16, 1863

Jane Ellen came by today. She brought bread and helped me with the wash.

Jane Ellen suggested that Pa visit the field hospitals outside of Gettysburg, between here and Uncle Jack's farm.

After she left, Pa told me he was going to hitch up Rex in the morning. He is going to look for Jed in the countryside.

I told him I must go with him. But he said no. He said he had seen too many terrible sights on his way to Gettysburg. He thinks I am too young to see such things.

July 18, 1863

This morning I made Pa change his mind. I grabbed his hands and held them tightly, so they wouldn't shake. I told him I had run away once from a terrible sight. I would never run away again. If we go to the hospitals, I will be extra brave, I said. For Jed's sake.

Pa said I sounded like my mother. He said she was very brave, too.

I told him I knew she was wishing we would both go look for Jed.

"All right, Elizabeth," Pa whispered, like he was talking to my mother and not me.

We will travel together now to every farmhouse, barn, stable, and schoolhouse to look for Jed.

Please wait, Jed. Please, please, wait for us.

July 19, 1863

It was a sunny day today. But no songbirds sang in the countryside. People say no songbirds have sung in the fields or woods since the roar of the cannons. Only vultures caw now.

Where did the songbirds go? Did they fly away? Or are they hiding in silence?

As Pa and I rode through the countryside, we saw dead men and rotting horses.

We saw broken fences, burned bridges, and destroyed crops.

We saw mounds of soldiers' graves. But no

soldier seems to have been buried decently. The graves are marked with just a bit of board — a slat from a barrel, a fence rail, a roof shingle. Names or initials are just scrawled on them in paint.

We came to a farm where the wagon shed, the pigsty, and barnyard were all crowded with wounded men. But Jed was not there.

We visited two other hospitals, both in farmhouses. But none of the men were Jed.

July 21, 1863

An astonishing thing happened today.

After a day of searching several field hospitals, we came upon one in a schoolhouse. I went in to ask about Jed, while Pa waited outside. He has become more and more distressed by the terrible suffering we have seen.

Inside, I discovered that most of the patients were Confederate soldiers. Many were so awfully sick they looked beyond all human aid.

But as I turned to leave, I heard someone call my name. It was Captain Heath! His head was bandaged.

I ran to the Confederate officer and shook his hand. He asked why I was there. I told him my father and I were looking for my brother Jed.

He said may God help us find him. He said he would pray that Jed is alive and unharmed.

Thank you, God, for keeping Captain Heath safe.

July 22, 1863

Pa has gone to bed, very weary. By the time we came home tonight, we had seen hundreds of wounded men.

At the last hospital, we met a kindly group of lady nurses from Philadelphia.

One asked me to help her dress a wound.

Pa kept urging me to come along, but I said I wanted to stay and help. I cut the bandage and wrapped it gently around a soldier's torn arm.

I am still horrified by the pain and suffering. I have not grown dead to my feelings. But I know one true thing about myself now — I will never run away from helping again.

July 24, 1863

It has been raining hard for two days. The creeks have overflowed, so we cannot take the buggy out.

Stay awake, Jed. Do not let God close your eyes. Do not sink into the long forever sleep.

July 26, 1863

The rain has stopped. But I fear Pa has lost hope for our search. He did not get out of bed yesterday or today.

I must go out alone. I told Pa I will ride Rex by myself tomorrow.

Pa did not say no. He is too worn down to think clearly. If he were well, I know he would not let me go alone.

July 27, 1863

I have stopped to let Rex rest for a moment before we head back to Gettysburg. I have ridden nearly all day.

At dawn, I started down Baltimore Pike, riding past the battlefields. They were silent and ghostly.

Still not a songbird sings.

I stopped at three hospitals on White Run and studied the wounded. None of them were Jed.

I stopped at a hospital in the village of Two Taverns. Jed was not there, either.

I must start for home now, to get back to Pa before dark.

Later

I will not be riding Rex home tonight. Pa will be worried.

But he will be happy to find out why.

On our ride down the pike, Rex was weary. We trotted through the twilight at a slow pace.

Near White Church Road, I heard a bird singing. It was the first bird I had heard in a long time.

It was not just a twitter. It was a wondrous song.

I stopped. I could not see the little bird in the brush. But its spirit moved me to turn Rex onto the road.

Shadows were falling quickly around the white church. A light burned in the open doorway.

I hitched Rex to a tree. When I looked inside the church, I saw dozens of men on beds of hay and straw. Lady nurses silently served from a soup kettle.

I asked one if I could look for my brother. She gave me a candle. I began carrying it from face to face.

Before I even came to Jed, my heart started to sing.

His eyes were closed. His face was hollow and pale. But I knew him at once. I knew the shape of his light brown beard, his lips, his long lashes. I knew his hands folded across his chest.

He has not seen me yet. He has not opened his eyes.

The nurses tell me Jed escaped from the Rebels and crawled here with a broken leg. He has a fever now and has slept for many days.

But Jed breathes. His heart beats.

I only have to wait for God to wake him up.

July 28, 1863

This morning one of the nurses will get word to Pa that Jed and I are here. I know he will come right away. I asked the nurse to tell him to bring *The Death of King Arthur* so I can read it to Jed.

Later

Pa is here. When he saw Jed was alive, he fell to his knees and wept with joy.

Now he is pacing back and forth beside the bed. He is watching Jed, anxious for him to wake up.

July 29, 1863

It is long after midnight. Pa snores now. But I still have not closed my eyes. I am afraid that if I stop seeing and hearing for Jed, he will slip away into that other world.

I have been talking to him of all the things he loves. I have reminded him of his books and his writing, of Pa and our mother and President Lincoln.

Still, he has not opened his eyes.

For the rest of the night, I will read to him from *The Death of King Arthur*.

Later

This is the brightest morning of our lives.

Did Jed hear me reading *The Death of King Arthur?*

Why else would he have opened his eyes just as I read: " . . . lightly and fiercely he pulled the sword out of the stone."?

That has always been his favorite part.

I laughed and cried to see him awake. So did Pa.

Jed was too weak to speak. He sleeps again now, but the nurse says his fever has broken.

I imagine that somewhere that little bird is singing its heart out.

July 31, 1863

Jed has been awake all morning.

Pa asked him about what happened, and

Jed told how he had been captured by Rebs on his way back to Gettysburg. He had escaped with two other prisoners. But he soon found himself in the midst of fighting. Jed was trampled by a horse and his leg was broken. As he lay on the ground, he saw the two men he had escaped with get killed by cannon fire.

When Jed started to speak of the death of his friends, he could not go on. He turned his face to the wall. He closed his eyes.

I tried to comfort him. I told him I had been his eyes and ears while he was gone. I asked if he wanted his journal back now.

He shook his head.

I asked if I should keep writing until he felt better.

He kept his eyes closed and nodded.

August 2, 1863

The doctor has just said magic words to us: He said Jed could go home this very afternoon.

Pa and the doctor will have to carry him to the buggy. He will not be able to walk at all for many months, the doctor said. In time, his broken leg should heal.

August 3, 1863

Jed is home safely. Right now I am in my bed, resting.

Jane Ellen and Mrs. McCully have just arrived. They have brought bread.

When Jane Ellen said hello to Jed, he barely even looked up. He did not seem to remember meeting her before.

I wish Jane Ellen could know the old Jed.

The one who laughed so easily and told good stories. This Jed seems only half here.

But I am glad Jane Ellen is visiting with him. I need to rest. I have not rested in a long time.

August 11, 1863

I am finally awake.

When I went to sleep, I slept for almost a week. I slept and slept and slept.

Jane Ellen told me that everyone grew worried about me. But I knew it was just my time to rest.

Jane Ellen helped keep our house while I slept.

Jed seems better. With Pa and Jane Ellen's help, he can get outside to the porch.

He does not talk much. But he seems to like watching the blue sky and feeling the warm sunlight.

August 14, 1863

I am sitting on top of Cemetery Hill.

This is the first time I have been here since the battle.

Many of the tombstones around me look wounded. They are chipped and riddled with holes.

My mother's, though, was not struck by even one bullet.

I think she is resting in peace again now that Jed and Pa and I are all safe together.

August 15, 1863

I am feeling very nervous.

Jed has asked me to read him my entries in his journal. I am worried that he will not like my writing. He might think it is too childish or simple.

Anyway, this will be my last entry, as I am certain he will want his journal back now. Thank you, Jed, for lending it to me.

Later

I am in heaven.

Jed listened very carefully as I read from his journal. He laughed when I read some parts. He looked very serious as I read others. Once I even saw him wipe tears from his eyes.

When I finished reading, he just stared at me for a long moment. Then he said I was a very good writer.

I could hardly breathe.

Jed said I should never stop writing. He said he wanted me to keep his journal and write in it every day.

I told him he should write in it himself.

Jed said he was done with writing for a

while. He said I was the writer in the family now.

I did not know what to say about that.

August 16, 1863

This morning, Jane Ellen came by again. She talked about her favorite books with me and Jed. She said she loves to read Sir Walter Scott's stories with their daring adventures.

Her face was aglow. I had never seen her look prettier.

It's odd that Jed never seems to take much notice of Jane Ellen. When I read my journal to him, I skipped over the parts about feeling cross with her. I think I had been a bit jealous.

I would have to say that I am not at all jealous of Jane Ellen anymore. Jed thinks I am a good writer. In his eyes, that is the very best thing in the world to be.

August 17, 1863

One of the Smith boys had a terrible accident today. He and some other boys were roaming the battlefields and found some shells. When the Smith boy picked one up, it went off in his face. He is not expected to live.

People from out of town also roam the battlefields. They are looking for souvenirs, such as cannonballs and cartridge boxes. They even take away dried mosses and twigs! Pa thinks they are being disrespectful of the dead.

August 19, 1863

Jed cried today.

He was reading to me, Pa, and Jane Ellen from *The Death of King Arthur*. It was the first time he has felt well enough to read.

In the middle of reading, he stopped and

just stared at the page. He was blinking hard. He seemed unable to catch his breath.

Jane Ellen asked him what was wrong.

In a halting, choked voice, Jed said that real battles were not like the battles in myths and legends. He said he did not understand why men did such terrible things to one another. He said that good men — not just terrible men — were capable of doing terrible things. This, Jed said, was the worst truth of all.

When Jed finished, time seemed to stand still. None of us spoke. There was only the sound of Jed weeping.

August 20, 1863

Today Jane Ellen gave Jed a new copy book. She gave him a new pen, too.

I stood in the doorway and watched her put them into his hands.

She told him that he must write. She spoke as if she were talking to a pupil.

Jed looked up at her with surprise.

"Write your thoughts about the war," she said firmly. "You must." Then she turned and left the room.

Jed stared after Jane Ellen, as if he had just seen her for the first time.

August 25, 1863

First day of school. A number of children were not present, including Betsy and Sally. Their families have not returned. Word has spread that Gettysburg is still blighted with death.

But I was there. So were the McHenry boys, the Wallace girls, Sue Peterson, and John Scott. And our new school mistress — Jane Ellen McCully.

How odd to have Jane Ellen for a teacher!

But I did not ask her for special attention or favors. In fact, I even called her "Miss Jane Ellen" while I was at school.

August 27, 1863

When I came home from school today, I was greeted with a wonderful sight and a wonderful sound.

I passed by Jed's room and saw him writing in the copy book Jane Ellen had given him.

Then I heard Pa playing his violin in his room. He was playing a tune I had never heard before. Several times he stopped and started over again. It sounded as if he were learning a new song.

August 30, 1863

I am sitting on top of Cemetery Hill. There is still a faint smell of death in the air. But today all the church bells in town rang again.

At our church, Reverend McCully said he thinks Gettysburg is starting to seem more like its old self. He said that more and more shops are opening back up, and some farmers are planting a late crop.

He said many buildings, though, will long show the scars of the battle. He has counted over 250 bullet holes in the trunk of one big tree near the battlefield.

Reverend McCully said the marks of the bullets should always remind us of those who died for the cause of freedom and union.

He also said that the battle of Gettysburg has turned the tide of the war against the Confederates.

September 5, 1863

I am again sitting on top of Cemetery Hill. The birds are singing. Indeed, the hilltop this afternoon is noisy with bird song.

Pa will go back to teaching his music lessons at the seminary tomorrow.

Jed often sits on the porch and writes in his copy book.

I give thanks every day that we are all together again and safe.

September 7, 1863

Jed called me and Pa into the parlor today. Jane Ellen was there with him.

Jed said he wanted to read to the three of us. He did not open *The Death of King Arthur*. Instead, he opened the copy book he had been writing in.

He began to read in a low voice. He read about how he had been captured, how he had escaped and been wounded, how he had crawled past countless dead men and horses.

Jed had written about many horrible things. But he had written in a clear and beautiful way. He wrote what he saw and what he heard. He wrote what he truly felt and what he truly thought about the war.

He said the war has shown that all citizens in this country — Northern and Southern — are capable of evil deeds. He said we are tied to our humanity by only a slender thread. So we must all strive every day to be more loving and kind.

When Jed was finished, all of us praised his wonderful writing.

Jane Ellen even said she wanted to share it with the McCullys and Mr. Hoke.

At first Jed said no.

But Jane Ellen was firm. She said everyone should hear his story.

September 16, 1863

Important news today.

Reverend McCully stopped by our school to announce that Governor Curtin is going to buy property near Gettysburg for a cemetery for the Union dead.

It will be on the north end of Cemetery Ridge — where the wheat field, apple orchard, and cornfield once were.

The bodies of Union soldiers will be removed from the shallow graves where they now lie. They will be given a proper burial in this sacred place. The new cemetery will be called the National Soldiers' Cemetery.

September 20, 1863

Jane Ellen brought more exciting news from Reverend McCully tonight. She told us there will be a ceremony in November to dedicate the National Soldiers' Cemetery.

The great orator Edward Everett will deliver a speech. Jane Ellen said that he is the best speaker in the nation. The governors of all the Northern states are invited, and cabinet members, and congressmen.

But the *most* exciting news is this: There will be another speaker at the ceremony.

It is President Abraham Lincoln himself!

We could not believe this news. President Lincoln is coming to Gettysburg!

October 21, 1863

I am on Cemetery Hill. This is the first time I have been here in several weeks.

My days are now filled with ordinary things — arithmetic, spelling, geography, and Latin. With so much schoolwork and chores, there has been little time to write in my journal.

Thankfully there has been little to report. No battles. No death.

October 23, 1863

Betsy returned to school today. I did not know what to say to her. I felt she was part of a life I used to have. Not my life since the battle.

October 28, 1863

Wonderful news.

Mr. Hoke showed Jed's story to his newspaper boss in Washington, D.C. The boss liked it very much! He wants to publish the whole story in his paper!

But the best news is this: When Jed gets well, the boss wants Jed to move to Washington and work as a writer for the newspaper!

After Mr. Hoke left, Jed called Pa and me into his room. He gave us the great news. But he said he would move to Washington only if Pa and I moved with him.

Pa seemed to like the idea. He thought he could get a job teaching music at a college. Perhaps he could even play his violin in one of the theaters in Washington.

As Pa and I were leaving Jed's room, Jed asked me to stay for a minute. He looked me in the eye and spoke very seriously. He said that if I kept writing, when I grew up I could write for a newspaper, too. He said it was all right to have two writers in the family. He said I was at least as good a writer as he.

Our life at this moment seems truly like a dream. I like to think my mother is spinning this dream for us.

November 7, 1863

Today Jane Ellen stopped me at the door of the schoolhouse. She asked if Mr. Hoke had come to our house last night.

I said yes. In a whisper, I told her the news about Jed's job in Washington.

Jane Ellen smiled knowingly. I realized then, of course, that she knew all about Mr. Hoke's offer to Jed.

Why, Jane Ellen was the one who had

caused it to happen! From start to finish. From the moment she gave Jed the copy book.

I told her that Jed wanted me and Pa to move to Washington with him.

Jane Ellen said she thought I would love Washington. Then a shadow crossed her face, and she fell silent.

I realized then that if Jed takes this job, he will not only be moving away from Gettysburg. He will also be moving away from Jane Ellen.

I must talk to him about this.

Later

After supper, I told Jed about my talk with Jane Ellen. I told him I was worried about her feelings.

He listened carefully, then sighed. He told me to stop by his room before I go to school in the morning. But he did not say why.

November 8, 1863

Before I went to school, Jed gave me a note to take to Jane Ellen. I promised not to read it.

I delivered it as soon as I got to the schoolhouse. Jane Ellen took it from me without a word. She pulled down the map of the United States. She told us all to choose a state and draw it, showing its capitol and major cities.

Then she slipped outside. I knew she wanted to be alone to read her note.

I started to draw Washington, D.C., even though I know it is not a state.

A moment later, the door opened. Jane Ellen stepped back into the room. Or should I say she nearly danced back into the room.

I knew at once something wonderful had happened.

I quickly drew a little house on my map of Washington, D.C. I labeled it "Our House," then drew four tiny people: Me, Pa, Jed, and Jane Ellen.

November 15, 1863

Late afternoon. I am sitting on Cemetery Hill.

A cold wind is sweeping over the grass. Finally the odor of death has left our town.

In a few days, more than 15,000 people are expected to be here for the dedication ceremony.

Sadly, Jed will not be able to attend. He has a cold. The doctor does not want him to risk getting pneumonia.

I burst into tears at the news that Jed would not be able to see President Lincoln. He tried to cheer me up. He told me he needed me to be his eyes and ears again. He told me to take my journal and write about the whole ceremony for him.

November 17, 1863

Today, we were dismissed from school so we could help clean and sweep the town for tomorrow's ceremony.

I pray I can get close enough to President Lincoln to write about him for Jed. I have learned that he will be staying at Judge Wills's house tomorrow night. Judge Wills's house is on the square, across from the Globe Hotel.

November 18, 1863

Pa and I are standing in the twilight, outside Judge Wills' house.

President Lincoln arrived a few minutes

ago. But the crowd was so thick we could not get close to him.

Pa held me up for a moment, so I could see the President step out of his carriage.

He is very tall with a black beard. His face has deep wrinkles.

He walked slowly, not looking at anyone. I watched him go into Judge Wills's house. Then the door was shut.

The crowd waited in the chilly dark and sang songs below his window.

An hour later

It is dark and cold now. People are still singing. Pa and I are still here, waiting. We are hoping the President will come out again.

Later still

The President is still inside the house. Pa thinks we should go home. He says that President Lincoln has likely retired for the night. He says the President must be giving deep thought to the words he will say tomorrow.

November 19, 1863

It is 10:30 in the morning. A heavy fog clouds the sky.

President Abraham Lincoln left Judge Wills's house a half hour ago. He is now riding a dark mare down Baltimore Street.

Following the President are Governor Curtin, two military bands, and many soldiers on foot and horseback.

The President is dressed in black and wears a high, silk hat.

Later

I am standing now with the McCullys, Jane Ellen, and Pa in the grass near the speaker's stand at the National Soldiers' Cemetery.

The sun is starting to shine through the clouds.

President Lincoln is seated. He looks very serious. He must feel the weight of the world upon him.

The Honorable Edward Everett is starting to speak. The crowd has grown perfectly silent.

Later

Mr. Everett is still speaking.

Later

Mr. Everett is still speaking.

Later

My goodness, Mr. Everett has been speaking for almost two hours!

Later

Hurrah! Finally Mr. Everett is sitting down.
The band plays music.
Now it is President Lincoln's turn to speak.
He puts on his glasses. He takes a crumpled piece of paper from his pocket.
He stands up. He looks at us. He speaks.

Later

President Lincoln's speech was very short.
When he finished, the crowd was a bit slow to applaud. I am not sure everyone understood that the President's speech was over.

But slowly the applause began to grow, until it was like a mighty wave.

I know you would have loved President Lincoln's speech, Jed. It was short. But it was honest and powerful. Just the way you told me to write.

November 20, 1863

The newspaper printed all of President Lincoln's Gettysburg Address. These are the lines I love the best:

Four score and seven years ago our fathers brought forth upon this continent, a new nation, conceived in liberty, and dedicated to the proposition that all men are created equal.

Now we are engaged in a great civil war, testing whether that nation, or any nation so conceived, and so dedicated, can long endure.

. . . we here highly resolve these dead shall not have died in vain, that this nation shall have a new birth of freedom, and that government of the people, by the people, for the people, shall not perish from the earth.

November 28, 1863

Tonight, the McCullys and Jane Ellen rode in the rain to our house. Mrs. McCully and Jane Ellen made a good meal of salt pork, yams, and biscuits.

After dinner, Jed called us all into the parlor. He and Jane Ellen were holding hands. They announced that they are engaged to be married.

Everyone was very happy. I think I was the happiest of all.

November 29, 1863

I am sitting on top of Cemetery Hill. A golden light bathes the freshly dug graves of those who died in the battle.

Last night Reverend McCully said there has been praise throughout the land for President Lincoln's Gettysburg Address.

He said that one magazine described the President's words best: They were from the heart to the heart.

President Lincoln hopes that those who died this summer did not die in vain. He is praying that this nation shall have a new birth of freedom, a nation of the people, by the people, and for the people.

He is praying that such a nation will never perish from the earth.

I think God listens to President Lincoln.

I think that people like President Lincoln,

Mrs. McCully, Mr. Hoke, Jane Ellen, Becky Lee, Captain Heath from the North Carolina mountains, Jed, and Pa will keep this nation from perishing from the earth.

I also think that children like me, who believe that all people are created equal, will keep this nation from perishing from the earth.

I might be bold to think that.

But that is truly what I think.

Historical Note

The Civil War was fought from 1861 to 1865. It is also called the "War Between the States," for the Northern and Southern states were at war with each other.

At the time of the Civil War there were many differences between the North and the South. The North had a more modern way of life. Many people lived in cities. Their economy was based on trade. The South had a rural way of life. They depended upon large plantations to grow sugar, cotton, and tobacco. Black slaves from Africa worked on these plantations.

Slaves work on a plantation in South Carolina in 1862.

The North had outlawed slavery. But Southerners thought their plantations couldn't exist without slaves. They wanted to make their own laws. So they decided to leave the "union" of the North and South. They formed the Confederate States of America. This led to the Civil War.

When the war had been going on for more than two years, General Robert E. Lee, commander of the Confederate army, led his men into Pennsylvania. He thought a victory in the North would be an important step to winning the war.

General Robert E. Lee on his famous horse, Traveler.

General Lee did not know that huge numbers of Union soldiers were also heading into Pennsylvania.

On July 1, almost 165,000 soldiers clashed in battle in the small farming town of Gettysburg, Pennsylvania. The battle lasted three days. It was the largest artillery battle ever fought on this continent.

Battle of Gettysburg—Charge of the Confederates on Cemetery Hill, Thursday Night, July 2, 1863.

A young soldier who fought in the Civil War.

The Union army won the battle. But the armies of both the North and the South suffered terrible losses in America's bloodiest war: A total of over 50,000 soldiers were killed, wounded, or missing.

The brave people of Gettysburg had no idea that they would ever find themselves in the midst of such a nightmare. When the battle was over, they were forced to

Union soldier Sergeant Amos Humiston died in the war. This photo of his children was found in his pocket.

bury all the dead and care for the wounded.

More than 3,000 women worked as nurses during the Civil War. Before the war, only men had been nurses. Here, a female nurse tends to the wounded, including a Confederate soldier, at Gettysburg.

Sixteenth President Abraham Lincoln.

The Battle of Gettysburg did not end the Civil War, which lasted another year and a half. But many historians see it as a turning point leading ultimately to the victory of the North. Fulfilling the dream of President Abraham Lincoln,

The people of the town of Gettysburg proceed to the dedication of the National Soldiers' Cemetery where President Lincoln delivered his powerful Gettysburg Address.

the United States became one nation again and slavery came to an end.

The most memorable speech ever made by an American president was Abraham Lincoln's Gettysburg Address, given in November 1863 at the dedication of the National Soldiers' Cemetery.

Generation after generation of Americans has revered President Lincoln's simple but powerful words:

"Four score and seven years ago our fathers brought forth upon this continent, a new nation, conceived in liberty, and dedicated to the proposition that all men are created equal.

"Now we are engaged in a great civil war, testing whether that nation or any nation so conceived, and so dedicated, can long endure. We are met on a great battle-field of that war. We have come to dedicate a portion of that field as a final resting place for those who here gave their lives that that nation might live. It is altogether fitting and proper that we should do this.

"But, in a larger sense, we can not dedicate — we can not consecrate — we can not hallow — this ground. The brave men, living and dead, who struggled here, have consecrated it, far above our poor power to add or detract. The world will little note, nor long remember what we say here, but it can never forget what they did here. It is for us the living, rather, to be dedicated here to the unfinished work which they who fought here have thus far so nobly advanced. It is rather for us to be here dedicated to the great task remaining before us—that from these honored dead we take increased devotion to that cause for which they gave the last full measure of devotion—that we here highly resolve that these dead shall not have died in vain—that this nation, under God, shall have a new birth of freedom—and that government of the people, by the people, for the people, shall not perish from this earth."

About the Author

Mary Pope Osborne says, "I'll never forget my trip to Gettysburg. Cemetery Hill seemed so strangely peaceful. Everything quiet, except for the wind in the grass and the *chur* of the crickets. It helped me understand how shocking the battle must have been to the people of that town."

Mary Pope Osborne is the award-winning author of more than forty books for children, among them the best-selling *Magic Tree House* series, *Adaline Falling Star*, and Dear America: *Standing in the Light: The Captive Diary of Catharine Carey Logan*. She lives with her husband, Will, in New York City.

Acknowledgments

The author would like to thank her editor, Amy Griffin, for her wonderful support. She would also like to thank Diane Garvey Nesin, Jean Feiwel, and the Gettysburg Visitor Center.

Grateful acknowledgment is made for permission to reprint the following:

Cover portrait and frontispiece by Glenn Harrington.

Page 101 (top): Slaves on plantation in South Carolina, 1862 by H.P. Moore, New-York Historical Society.

Page 101 (bottom): General Robert E. Lee on his famous horse, Traveler, Brown Brothers, Sterling, Pennsylvania.

Page 102: Battle of Gettysburg, ibid.

Page 103 (top): A soldier in the Civil War, Library of Congress.

Page 103 (bottom): The children of a Union soldier, The J. Howard Wert Gettysburg Collection.

Page 104 (top): A hospital in the Civil War, Atlanta History Center.

Page 104 (bottom): Abraham Lincoln, Brown Brothers, Sterling, Pennsylvania.

Page 105: People of Gettysburg proceeding to dedication of National Soldiers' Cemetery, Library of Congress.

For Gail Hochman,
with the deepest gratitude.

⊹⟫☰⟩ ⟨☰⟨⊹

While the events described and some of the characters in this book may be based on actual historical events and real people, Virginia Dickens is a fictional character, created by the author, and her diary is a work of fiction.

Library of Congress Cataloging-in-Publication Data Available

ISBN 0-439-15307-7

10 9 8 7 6 5 4 3 2   0/0 01 02 03 04 05

Photo research by Zoe Moffitt
Book design by Elizabeth B. Parisi
Printed in the U.S.A. 23
First edition, June 2000

⊹⟫☰⟩ ⟨☰⟨⊹

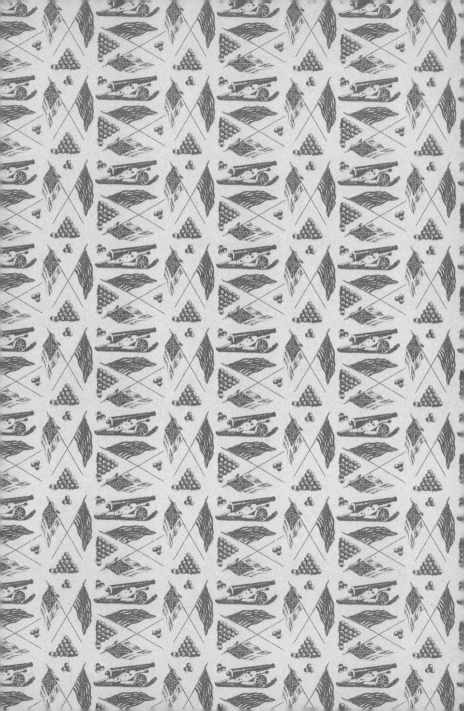